Making Happy

written by
Sheetal Sheth

illustrated by
Khoa Le

Barefoot Books
step inside a story

"Leila? Leila? Are you sure you don't want to share anything for our 'How Can I Help?' project?" Mrs. Kreisman asked gently.

Leila shook her head. She didn't feel like it. She didn't feel like doing much of anything lately.

Leila had an ache in her stomach that would not go away.
The kind that lingered long through the day, even after
she'd had her fill of a delicious ice-cream sundae.

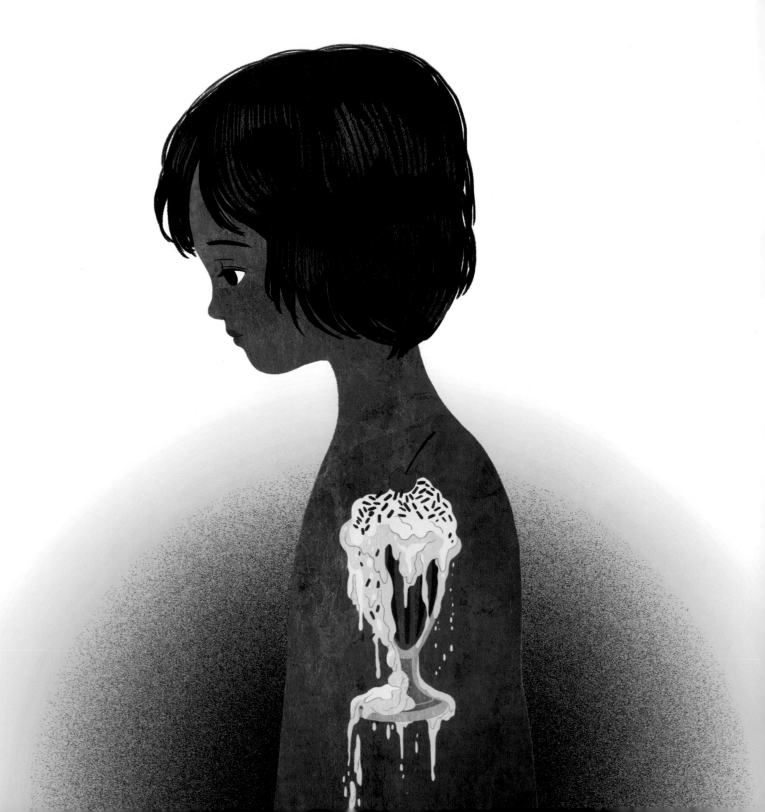

So much was changing.
Her mama took a lot of naps lately.

Mama had a wig now too. And a lot of scarves. Leila wished Mama would wear the wig more often. She didn't like how people looked at Mama without it.

"Hair doesn't make someone beautiful. Being kind does," Mama always said.

Leila liked picking out which scarf Mama was going to wear. Sometimes Leila wore one too and they pretended they were rulers of the universe. Mama would whisper, "We are all goddesses. Never forget that."

Leila had a lot of play dates. After
school, she would go home with her friend
Sloane. Sloane had a tent. They would sit in
the dark and make wishes on the stars.

Leila always wished for her
family to go back to normal.

One time, Mama was coughing so much she had to go to the hospital. Leila didn't understand why Mama couldn't come home for three days. And she was really angry that Mama missed her solar system presentation.

Leila tried to make the sick go away.

She did her homework.

She ate her carrots.

She picked all her clothes up off the floor.

She even prayed although she didn't really know if she was doing it right or who she was talking to.

One evening, Leila and her dad were eating dinner
when Leila abruptly knocked over her glass.
She stared at the water as it
spilled over the table
and onto the floor.

Suddenly she
burst into tears.

They wouldn't
stop.

Leila felt Dad wrap his arms around her. He didn't let her go. Dad was crying too. Leila said, "Sorry, Dad. I'm so sorry. I don't know why I did that. Are you mad?"

Dad kissed her and said, "Of course not! None of us are feeling like ourselves lately. You know what we need? We need to make some happy!"

"Make happy?" Leila asked.

"Yes! The bigger the mess, the better!"
Dad said in a silly voice. "Right, Mama?"

"That's right! Let's do it!" Mama
said while Dad put on some music.

Leila watched
with wide eyes.

Music filled the room as Dad started tearing up newspapers.
Leila's feet started tapping to the beat.
Mama grabbed some pillows. "Leila, come and join in!"

They danced and twirled.
They punched the pillows until the room was covered in feathers.
It was the most dazzling mess Leila had ever seen.

They looked at each other
and started laughing.

And then they talked . . .
long into the night.

As Leila fell asleep between her parents, she felt herself floating.

She drifted until she landed on the ocean.
Her feet settled among the waves as she found her balance.
It was silent. She was alone with nothing in sight.

Except one bird.

The bird was flailing and clearly in pain.

Leila noticed a piece of seaweed tangled around its legs.

Leila carefully removed it.

Leila stayed and watched quietly.
The bird wouldn't give in.

Then, she heard a sound. The bird's voice —
faint at first, but then louder and louder
until the ocean air was echoing with a glimmering joy.

The bird was singing through the pain.
Leila was too. And it was exquisite.

Leila woke up bursting with energy. The ache in her stomach was gone.

At school, she raised her hand for the first time in weeks. "Could I take a turn for the 'How Can I Help?' project?"

"Of course!" Mrs. Kreisman said.

"Well . . . my mama is sick right now and she has to rest a lot. I was thinking I'd like to make a quilt for her."

"Thank you for sharing, Leila. That's such a thoughtful idea," Mrs. Kreisman said.

"Could I help?" John asked shyly.

"I'd like to help too!" Daya said.

"Me too! Me too!" Satya chimed in.

"How about we all help?
What do you think, class?"
Mrs. Kreisman asked with a smile.

One evening, Leila asked softly, "Mama, why did you get sick?"

Mama answered, "I don't know, love."

"Is it because you're strong?" Leila mused.

"Maybe." Mama smiled. "Probably."

"But why did it have to be you?" Leila pressed.

"Well, why not me? Someone else wouldn't have you."

And as they sat there together, the stillness in Leila
gave rise to an ocean of feeling, full of might.
Leila's heart was steady, brave
and ready to sing.

To those we lost too soon, to fellow warriors who fight so tough and so deep, and to my lovelights who show me the way — S. S.

For Mom and Dad, who know making happy in their own way — K. L.

Author's Note

This book is a love letter to anyone struggling. I wrote this book when I was looking for a little happy for me and my family. I was in the throes of chemotherapy, my children were quite young and we were trying to process everything that comes with a cancer diagnosis. Drowning in a sea of well-intentioned "everything is going to be okay," "be strong" or "things happen for a reason," what I wanted and needed most was to feel whatever I felt. Our children have more to deal with than ever and need to know that it's okay to have big feelings — to be sad, scared and angry. We expect our kids to be resilient and strong, yet we don't talk about how. I hope this book allows for conversations that are as honest and raw as we each need. And ultimately that it leaves you with a little hope, a little peace and a whole lot of love.

— Sheetal Sheth

Illustrator's Note

I work mostly digitally, with some personal touches of traditional media and photography. I create texture with water-based paints, oil paints or mixed media. I love to travel, so I enjoy photo-hunting for patterns in nature. I love fabric patterns too and I try to use fabrics related to the author's heritage to bring something unique to each book.

I love this story because of how real it feels, yet there is also the lightness of hope and joy. I thought there was no better way to deliver that message than by bringing lots of vibrant, lively details into the illustrations, but I also tried to limit my palette in certain moments that convey the sadness the characters feel. I think in life, all those elements are important: happiness, sadness, hopes, dreams, disappointment, joy … without any one of those, we cannot have the others. It takes bravery to learn to embrace it all.

— Khoa Le

Barefoot Books, 23 Bradford Street, 2nd Floor, Concord, MA 01742
Barefoot Books, 29/30 Fitzroy Square, London, W1T 6LQ

Text copyright © 2022 by Sheetal Sheth. Illustrations copyright © 2022 by Khoa Le
The moral rights of Sheetal Sheth and Khoa Le have been asserted

First published in the United States of America by Barefoot Books, Inc
and in Great Britain by Barefoot Books, Ltd in 2022. All rights reserved

Graphic design by Sarah Soldano, Barefoot Books
Edited and art directed by Lisa Rosinsky, Barefoot Books
Reproduction by Bright Arts, Hong Kong. Printed in China
This book was typeset in Albemarle and Catalina Clemente
The illustrations were prepared digitally with touches of traditional media and photography

Hardback ISBN 978-1-64686-622-9 | Paperback ISBN 978-1-64686-623-6
E-book ISBN 978-1-64686-705-9

British Cataloguing-in-Publication Data: a catalogue record for this book
is available from the British Library

Library of Congress Cataloging-in-Publication Data is available under LCCN 2022008110

135798642

For more "Making Happy" tips and ideas for coping with big feelings, visit www.barefootbooks.com/making-happy.

Barefoot Books
Step inside a story

At Barefoot Books, we celebrate art and story that opens the hearts
and minds of children from all walks of life, focusing on themes that
encourage independence of spirit, enthusiasm for learning and respect
for the world's diversity. The welfare of our children is dependent on
the welfare of the planet, so we source paper from sustainably managed
forests and constantly strive to reduce our environmental impact.
Playful, beautiful and created to last a lifetime, our products combine
the best of the present with the best of the past to educate our
children as the caretakers of tomorrow.

www.barefootbooks.com

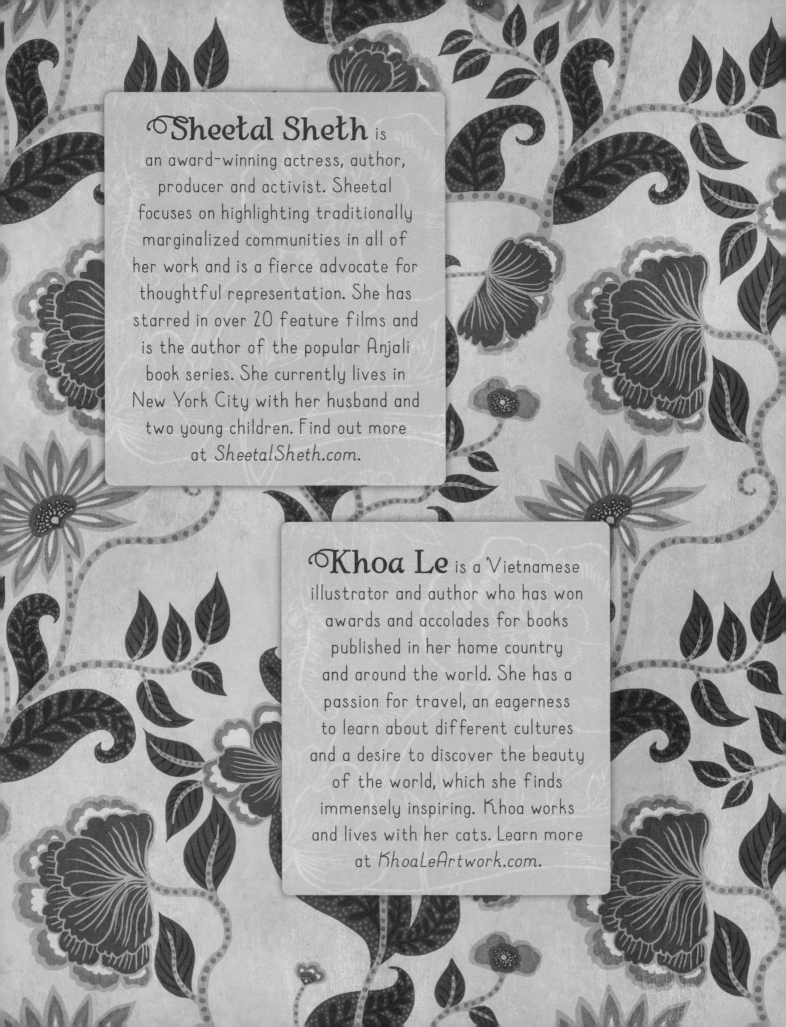

Sheetal Sheth is an award-winning actress, author, producer and activist. Sheetal focuses on highlighting traditionally marginalized communities in all of her work and is a fierce advocate for thoughtful representation. She has starred in over 20 feature films and is the author of the popular Anjali book series. She currently lives in New York City with her husband and two young children. Find out more at *SheetalSheth.com*.

Khoa Le is a Vietnamese illustrator and author who has won awards and accolades for books published in her home country and around the world. She has a passion for travel, an eagerness to learn about different cultures and a desire to discover the beauty of the world, which she finds immensely inspiring. Khoa works and lives with her cats. Learn more at *KhoaLeArtwork.com*.